Flightless

Diana Noonan

Contents

Birds That Do Not Fly

All birds have wings and feathers.
But some birds cannot fly.
They are called "flightless birds".

Birds that can fly have strong, light wings.

Many birds that cannot fly
have very small wings.

Flightless birds live all over the world.

Finding Food

Lots of birds that can fly
find food to eat in the **treetops**.

But most flightless birds cannot do this.
They have to find their food on the ground.
Some hunt for food in the sea.

Nests

Most birds that can fly make nests in trees.

Many flightless birds make their nests on or near the ground.

Big Flightless Birds

Some flightless birds are very big.
They cannot fly away from **predators**.
Their wings are too small.

But they can run away,
because they have long, strong legs.
They can run very fast.

The Ostrich

The ostrich is a big flightless bird from South Africa.
It has long legs and a very long neck.
It can see over the top of tall grass.

The ostrich watches for predators with its big eyes.

The Emu

The emu is the biggest bird in Australia.
It cannot fly, because it has very small wings.

The emu is a fast runner.
It will chase any animal that comes near its eggs.

The Rhea

The rhea is the biggest bird in South America.
Its little wings help **steer** it
when it is running fast.

The rhea makes a nest on the ground.
It will chase away predators
that try to take its eggs.

Small Flightless Birds

Many small flightless birds live in New Zealand.

Small flightless birds are clever at hiding from predators.

The Kiwi

The kiwi is a flightless bird.
It lives in the New Zealand forests.
Its brown feathers help it
to hide from predators.

The kiwi comes out at night.
It is very good at smelling food
with its long **beak**.

The Kakapo

The kakapo is a flightless bird.
It lives on the forest floor, in New Zealand.
Its feathers are green like the trees.

The kakapo can climb trees to find food.
It keeps very still when a predator is close.

There are not many kakapo left in New Zealand.

Penguins

Penguins are flightless birds.

They live in many places around the world.

Not all penguins look the same.

Some are big and some are very small.

Penguins are strong and can swim very fast.

Some penguins make nests on the cold ground.
Others make their nests in **burrows**.

Looking After Flightless Birds

Flightless birds are not always safe.
They are often run over on roads
by cars and other traffic.
Wild cats hunt flightless birds
in the forests.

Lots of people work hard
to care for flightless birds,
their eggs and their chicks.

Where Flightless Birds Live

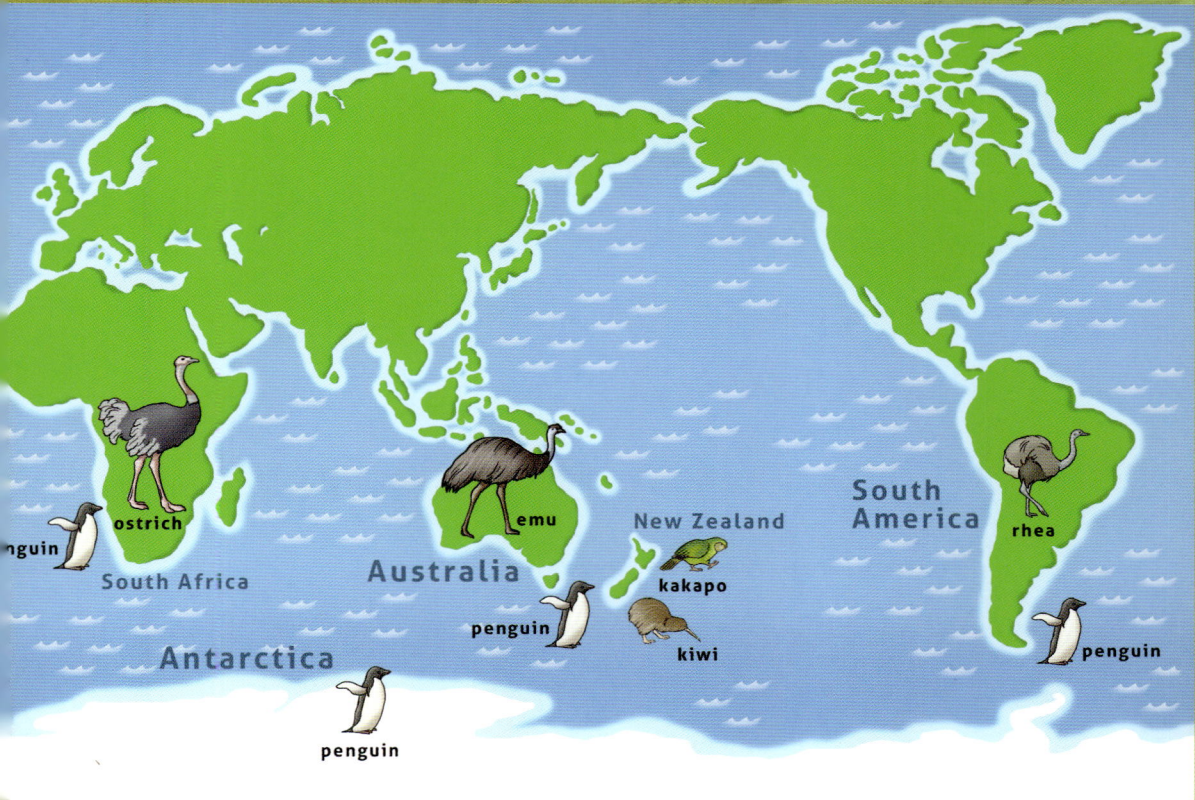

ostrich

penguin

South Africa

Antarctica

penguin

emu

Australia

penguin

New Zealand

kakapo

kiwi

South America

rhea

penguin

Glossary

beak   the hard part of a bird's mouth

burrows   holes in the ground
                  that some animals and birds live in

predators   animals that hunt other animals
                  for food

steer   to make something move this way
                  or that way

treetops   the top parts of trees